LOCKDOWN *memories*

Toby finds a mask

Book-1

Written by David Bannister

Toby's Adventures

Toby Finds A Mask

Book-1

The Gate is left open

Toby sat in the garden watching the butterflies and bees flying by.

He suddenly noticed the garden gate was open.

"I wonder what happens beyond the gate?" thought Toby.

Toby went on his first adventure. He was very excited and as he went, his nose started to sniff new smells and his ears picked up new sounds.

Toby found a tin with his picture on it. He picked it up and carried it home.

He told everyone he met on the way that he was famous because his photo was on the fizzy drinks tin.

Toby was feeling pleased with himself.

On the way home Toby found out it wasn't him on the tin. It was a Polar Bear who was the same colour as him.

Toby found a rubbish bin and put the tin in the recycle bin.
Toby was feeling sad.
Later with the gate still open, Toby went exploring again.

Toby went out of the gate again and it wasn't long before he came across what he thought was a snake but there were no wiggles in this snake, which was actually just a long stick.

Toby brought it home but as it was too long, he could not get it through the gate. Toby dropped the stick where he had found it.

Toby was not giving up. He was sure he would find something important, so off he went, out through the gate. It wasn't long before he found something that he was sure would be important.

Toby found a little toy yellow pig and carried it back home in his mouth.

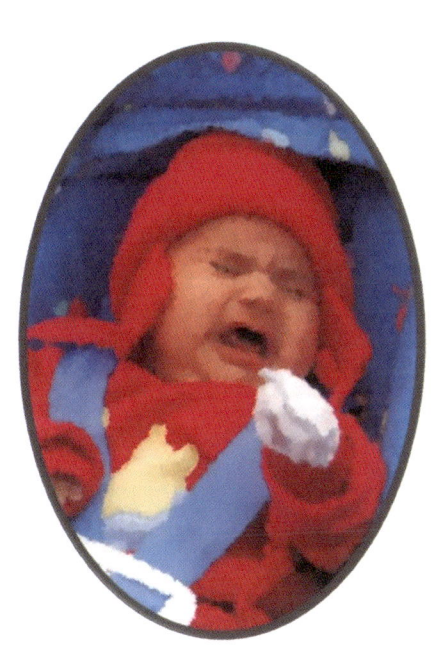

Toby got a shock when he arrived home.

He found a little baby crying because he had lost his new toy yellow pig.

The Baby must have dropped it out of the pram.

Toby decided he had just enough time for one more adventure out through the gate.
It wasn't long before he discovered a strange object lying on the ground.

He picked it up and realised he had seen people wearing these so he tried it on.

Toby noticed people were laughing at him.

He thought to himself, "Maybe I'm wearing it wrong," so he tried another way of wearing it.

People were still laughing.

Toby looked at other people and suddenly he realised what was funny.
Toby put the mask on the same way other people were wearing theirs.

Toby arrived back at his gate and he was now contented he had got it right.

People were telling him he was a clever dog and soon all the dogs in the neighbourhood were wearing their masks properly.

Printed in Great Britain
by Amazon